Bomba
the Brave

By Denise Dufala

Illustrated by Kimberly Soderberg

Halo
PUBLISHING
INTERNATIONAL

For James, Jonathan, and Mrs. Fish.
-D. D.

For my parents, who taught me to be brave.
-K. S.

Copyright © 2018 Denise Dufala
Illustrated by Kimberly Soderberg
All rights reserved.

Summary: Bomba and his friends learn to be kind and stick together.

ISBN: 978-1-61244-642-4
Library of Congress Control Number: 2018904093

Printed in the United States of America

Halo Publishing International
1100 NW Loop 410
Suite 700 - 176
San Antonio, Texas 78213
Toll Free 1-877-705-9647
www.halopublishing.com
e-mail: contact@halopublishing.com

Foreword

We live in an era when parents are wondering how to raise their children to be decent people. Children will be exposed to many conflicting messages and temptations as they grow. They will see acts of violence on television and in movies. Peer pressure, social media and many other influences will clutter their heads. What will compel them to be brave and moral, to lift others up? There is no simple solution.

Parents and teachers must sort through the puzzle pieces and select those that, when assembled in the minds of children, will guide their actions and set them on the right path. Courage, compassion, kindness, honesty, and tenacity are among the pieces that will lift children up when they're down, and hold them back when their egos are inflated. *Bomba the Brave* represents the character and values that will complement the puzzle pieces parents and teachers assemble. Through the illustrated character Bomba the Bunny, my friend and colleague Denise Dufala helps parents raise children who will be good and do good. Bomba is one of the impressions that can aid the moral development of children.

Stuart Muszynski
President & CEO Values-In-Action Foundation

The first day of school, as exciting as can be.
A special day indeed for Bomba Zurawski.

Bomba is a bunny who loves to jump and sing.

His favorite is the hopscotch song,
it has a certain ring.

"Hippity hopscotch 1 and 2.
That's what bunnies love to do.
Hippity hopscotch 3 and 4.
Jumping higher makes you soar!"

Bomba hopped right out the door, happily on his way.
"Be kind to others dear," called Mom. "Be a friend. Be brave."

Bomba couldn't help but shout,
"I'm Bomba the brave."
He took a carrot from his pouch,
and gave his mom a wave.

He raced so fast down the lane, singing all the way.
Summer was finally over, and now the big first day!

A new year, a new desk, he was sure to meet new friends.
He never could have dreamed how this first day would end.

His turn came up to read aloud and suddenly he froze. He couldn't see the writing much farther than his nose!

Be brave, he thought. He tried again. The letters all looked funny.
"What's the matter, can't you read?" Laughed Ben, the biggest bunny.

Bomba looked around the class
hoping for some help. All he heard
was laughter. All he could do was yelp.

"Now class," said Mrs. Fish towards Ben,
"don't laugh. You know it's cruel. Bomba take
a seat, my dear. I'll see you after school."

Bomba was embarrassed. He no longer felt brave.
He wished that he could disappear and crawl into a cave.

When recess came, Bomba thought
that would bring relief.

15

It did, until Ben came around
and caused him lots of grief!

"Hippity hopscotch 1, 2, 3.
Bomba's up, but he can't see!
Hippity hopscotch 4 and 5.
Jump with him, you'll take a dive!"

Now the other bunnies were feeling kind of sad.
What Ben was doing to Bomba made them kind of mad.

Bomba was their buddy. He was extra nice.
But if they tried to help him, they could pay the price.

The final bell found Momma
bunny right outside the door.
Bomba leaped into her arms,
and down, the tears did pour.

"My dear," said Mrs. Fish to
Mom, "it's pretty clear to me.
Bomba needs a doctor,
the kind to help him see."

So they went to Doctor Otter,
an expert in the field. He tested
Bomba's eyes. The problem, soon revealed.

Bomba needed glasses to help him see things far. He liked
the way they made him feel just like a movie star.

The next day Bomba noticed how much prettier things looked.
The best part, he could see the board and every single book.

At recess Bomba hopped into
the hopscotch extra high.

23

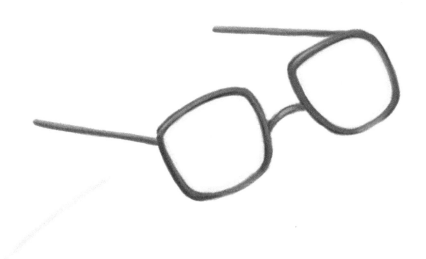

He didn't know his cool new specs could fall right off and fly.

In jumped Ben pretending he was in the hopscotch games.
He hopped until he heard a crunch, and there went Bomba's frames!

They broke right down the middle. Cracked 'em right in two.
However could he mend them? Perhaps a little glue?

A friendly girl came up to help. She knew a thing or two.
She wrapped them up with duct tape, almost better than brand new!

The kids all knew this handy girl. They called her Tiny Tess.
She wasn't afraid to say something when someone made a mess.

"Ben, you need to stop it,
and learn to be more kind."
And when the class heard Tess
speak up, they all felt peace of mind.

The bunnies started cheering. They put Ben in his place.
If they could stick together, he'd be easier to face.

Ben sat on the sidelines. He knew that he'd done wrong. Boy was he relieved when Bomba sang their favorite song.

"Hippity hopscotch 1, 2, 3.
Come on Ben and jump with me.
Hippity hopscotch 4 and 5.
Jumping makes you feel alive!"

After everything that happened, Bomba was a friend.
Ben leaped right in to join him with a new message to send.

**"Hippity hopscotch 1 and 2.
That's what bunnies love to do.
Hippity hopscotch 3 and 4.
All together we can soar!"**

Denise Dufala is an Emmy-award-winning journalist who spent 30 years as a news anchor and reporter at the CBS affiliate in Cleveland, Ohio. She also wrote a page 2 column for the Sunday edition of the Cleveland Plain Dealer. Denise is a member of the Ohio Radio-Television Broadcasters Hall of Fame, and the Cleveland Association of Broadcasters Hall of Fame. She is also a member of the Society of Children's Book Writers and Illustrators (SCWBI).

In 2017, Denise teamed up with Values-In-Action Foundation to become National Program Ambassador for their school-based anti-bullying program, *Be Kind*™ STICK TOGETHER.™

Denise is known for her work with children and charities. She regularly volunteers for The Make-A-Wish Foundation, and sings in her church choir. Bomba the Brave is Denise's first book. It is based on a story she wrote in the first grade, as a student of Mrs. Kathy Fish. Denise resides in Cleveland, Ohio with her husband Ed and their son, James, who created the first illustration of Bomba.

Kimberly Soderberg lives in Cleveland, Ohio, with her husband and two sons, who provide her with continuous inspiration. Her love of drawing started in early childhood. As a little girl, Kim carried around a box with paper and pencils wherever she went, and often drew pictures of her pet bunny, Hopper.

She studied at the Columbus College of Art & Design where she received her bachelor's degree in Fine Arts, with an emphasis in Illustration. After graduation she joined the Society of Children's Book Writers and Illustrators (SCWBI), and dedicated herself to learning all there is to know about the art of children's illustration.

Since then she has worked with a number of clients including Scholastic, Oxford University Press, Creative Teaching Press, and Bauer Media Group.

CPSIA information can be obtained
at www.ICGtesting.com
Printed in the USA
LVHW071455010219
606088LV00019B/294/P